QREADS

THE KULA'I
STREET KNIGHTS

JANET LORIMER

SADDLEBACK
EDUCATIONAL PUBLISHING

Q READS

SADDLEBACK
EDUCATIONAL PUBLISHING
www.sdlback.com

ISBN-13: 978-1-61651-182-1
ISBN-10: 1-61651-182-6
eBook: 978-1-60291-904-4

Printed in Malaysia

21 20 19 18 17   4 5 6 7 8

■ ■ ■

Eddie gazed into a sea of angry faces. The men and women gathered in the Kalihi Community Center were people he'd known all his life. But tonight, their fear and frustration made them seem like strangers.

"—Why can't you do something?" Everyone was talking at once, so Eddie heard only part of what Mr. Chang was asking. But he could easily figure out the rest. Everyone in the Center was wondering the same thing. *Why can't you protect us, Eddie Kahele? You're a cop!*

He held up his hands for silence. Bit by bit the talking stopped.

"Mr. Chang," Eddie said patiently, "I'm

only one cop. This neighborhood is not the only trouble spot in Honolulu. That's why you folks need to form a Neighborhood Watch. You have to look out for each other."

Mr. Chang made a disgusted face. "I grew up in Kalihi," the old man said. "We had gangs when I was a kid—but not like what we have today. Back then, kids were mischievous, not vicious or even mean. Things are worse now."

"I know," Eddie said quickly. "Things have changed a lot. But that's not what we're here to talk about. Let's stay on the subject, please."

An elderly woman in the front row stood up. Eddie smiled to himself. Auntie Malia had seemed old when he was little, but now she really was old! She was also one of his favorite aunties. Not that she and Eddie were related by blood. In Hawaii, young people called their elders "auntie" and "uncle" out of respect.

"Eddie," she said, "I'm too old to patrol the streets. What can I do to help?"

Eddie explained that not everyone had to go out on patrol. He talked about block captains. He explained how the people in the neighborhood could look out for each other. But he could see it was a lost cause. By the time the meeting was over, only a handful of people had signed up for the Neighborhood Watch.

When Eddie left the Center, he felt frustrated. Deep in thought, he headed for his small apartment a couple of blocks away.

A full moon splashed silver light over the monkeypod trees that lined the street. The warm air was sweet with the lemony scent of plumeria blossoms. As he walked, Eddie remembered being a kid here, playing ball in the street on nights like this. In those days he hadn't had a care in the world.

Then he grew up, and the world changed.

Hawaii had breathtaking rainbows, beautiful beaches, and perfumed air—but it was not really paradise. Honolulu had the same problems as any other big city. Kalihi was an old neighborhood, a poor neighborhood. But people of all different races lived, worked, and played here together. Eddie loved that. As far back as he could remember, living in Kalihi meant having a sense of "ohana"—a feeling of family.

Kalihi had always had its share of crime. Now and then, kids ripped off something from Mr. Chang's little grocery store. Sometimes a car got stolen for a joy ride. But for the most part, the gangs were a nuisance, not a threat.

Then the face of crime began to change. The criminals started packing knives and guns. And stealing wasn't enough. They seemed to get a thrill out of beatings and killings. They respected no one and nothing. In fact, just a week ago, old Mrs. Shiroma had been badly beaten after cashing her pension check. She had stubbornly refused to hand over the money to her attacker.

Eddie was thinking about Mrs. Shiroma when a loud scream ripped through the night. He froze, trying to figure out where the sound had come from. Then he heard men's voices raised in anger and the sounds of fighting. Eddie tore down the street and into a narrow alley.

It was pitch black. Eddie had to slow his pace. Halfway down the alley, he tripped over a trash can. Luckily he caught himself before he fell, and kicked the can to one side. The sound of metal scraping asphalt echoed in the night air.

When Eddie reached the mouth of the alley, he saw Auntie Malia and the shadowy figures of four men. Eddie yelled, hoping to distract them. At the sound of his voice, the figures vanished into the shadows.

Eddie hurried to Auntie Malia. The old woman was shaking from head to toe. She clung to Eddie's arm as she talked excitedly. "It was unreal, Eddie. Three young *kolohe*—rascals—tried to knock me over and steal my purse. But then four guys came out of nowhere to help me. They *saved* me, Eddie!"

Eddie shook his head, trying to make sense of what Auntie was telling him. "Who—" he started to say, but Auntie Malia went on excitedly.

"They said they were the Kula'i Street Knights. I never heard of that gang before."

Neither had Eddie. And he wasn't sure he liked what he was hearing. The trouble was Auntie. As far as she was concerned, these Street Knights were angels sent from heaven.

■ ■ ■

When Eddie arrived at the station the next morning, he told his sergeant all about the incident. Sgt. Amosa shrugged. "Not much we can do unless your auntie fingers the punks who tried to rob her. All the same, keep your eyes and ears open. Let's just hope these guys aren't outsiders moving in to start a gang war."

Eddie nodded. "What I can't figure out is why they stopped to *help* an old woman."

The sergeant shook his head and grinned. "Maybe heroism is back in fashion," he said sarcastically.

Eddie raised one eyebrow. "Yeah—and maybe I'm going to Vegas next weekend and win a million bucks."

Both men burst out laughing.

Eddie didn't think much more about the Street Knights that morning. But when he stopped for lunch at a local diner, everyone there was talking about the denim-clad angels. The story of Auntie's rescue had spread through the neighborhood like wildfire.

"Eddie, did you hear?" Mr. Apana said as he wiped the counter. The diner was old. The paint was faded, and the plastic-covered stools were mended with tape. But Mr. Apana made the best plate lunch in Kalihi.

"Did you hear how those Street Knights saved Auntie Malia?" Mr. Apana went on. The old man was grinning. Eddie noticed that everyone else in the diner was nodding and smiling, too.

Eddie nodded. "I was there when it happened," he said. "I'm just glad that Auntie wasn't hurt."

Then Mrs. Apana handed Eddie his favorite plate lunch—teriyaki beef, two scoops of rice, and macaroni salad. Eddie lifted a big bite of teriyaki beef with his chopsticks. In spite of everyone's enthusiasm over the Street Knights, he couldn't shake the feeling that something about these heroes was just plain *wrong*.

"No need now for a Neighborhood Watch," someone said. Eddie glanced over his shoulder. Other folks in the diner were nodding in agreement.

Eddie spun around on the stool. "Look," he said firmly, "just because these guys helped Auntie doesn't mean they'll help anyone else. If they're so wonderful, why did they run off before I could talk to them?"

Their smiles quickly disappeared. It was as if the temperature in the room had dropped. Eddie could feel the people's hostility.

"Come on, Eddie, cut it out," Mrs. Apana scolded. "How come you have to find fault with everything? Those boys saved Malia, and that's that."

Eddie sighed, swung back around on the

stool, and went on eating. He knew it would do no good to argue. The neighborhood people *wanted* to believe that they had a team of guardian angels looking out for them.

That afternoon at work, Eddie kept thinking about the incident from the night before. Why hadn't the four men hung around? Maybe they had records and were afraid he would recognize them. Who *were* they? Just another gang moving into the neighborhood? Eddie sighed. That didn't make sense, either. Gang members didn't bother to save little old ladies.

Later, while he was filing some reports, he heard a loud commotion. Sgt. Amosa stuck his head around the door. "Hey, Eddie, you might want to hear this," he said.

Eddie raised an eyebrow. "About—?"

"Mr. Fernandez just got mugged. He came in to report it. He says he was on his way home when three guys stopped him. They threatened to hurt him if he didn't hand over his wallet. Then all of a sudden, out of nowhere, four more guys appear. They tell the first guys to beat it—to leave the old man alone. The muggers supposedly put up a fight—"

"*Supposedly?*" Eddie cut in.

The sergeant nodded. "From what Mr. Fernandez says, it didn't sound like much of a tussle. No one used a weapon. No one got hurt. After a little scuffle the perps just ran away."

Eddie's frown deepened. Amosa's grin widened. "Then—and this is the good part—these guys say to Fernandez, 'You folks don't have to be scared any more. We're the Kula'i Street Knights. We're here to help you clean up your neighborhood and make it safe.'"

Eddie shook his head in disbelief. "You're kidding!"

The sergeant leaned against the door-jamb. "They didn't ride off on white horses," he went on, "but as far as Mr. Fernandez is concerned, those guys are heroes with a capital *H*."

Eddie followed Amosa to the cubicle where Mr. Fernandez was telling his story to another officer. Mr. Fernandez wasn't elderly, but he had been disabled a few months before in a construction accident. His obvious disability made him an easy target for muggers.

When Mr. Fernandez saw Eddie, his smile vanished. "You cops tell all of us neighbors to form a Neighborhood Watch. You tell us to patrol the streets. So what good are *you*?"

Eddie winced.

The sergeant stepped into the middle of it. "Sorry you feel that way," he told Mr. Fernandez. "We're doing the best job we can—but our hands are tied, too. We have to follow procedure and the law. Guys like these Street Knights don't."

Mr. Fernandez began to cool down. He looked a little sheepish. "Sorry," he muttered. "Guess I shot my mouth off."

He gave the cops a description of the three men who had tried to mug him. As Eddie listened, he flashed back on what Auntie Malia had said about the punks who'd tried to mug her. The descriptions matched.

■ ■ ■

Within a couple of days, Eddie gave up any hope of forming a Neighborhood Watch. As he walked around the neighborhood, he heard more and more people talking about their new defenders. The Street Knights saved people and wanted nothing in return. It seemed almost too good to be true.

When Eddie tried to point this out, people jumped all over him. The Knights, they said, were only doing what the cops should have been doing all along!

One evening, Eddie was on his way home from the Community Park. He coached an after-school soccer team there, and tonight's practice had run late. As he walked down the street he was lost in thought, his fists thrust deep into his pockets. His head was down as he walked along.

Then Eddie was caught off-guard by a hard blow between his shoulder blades. Down he went, face-first onto the concrete, the breath knocked out of him. Someone pulled his arms up behind his back. Pain shot through his body.

"Check his pockets," he heard a rough male voice say. "Look for his gun."

Eddie felt himself being searched. "Nothing," another voice said.

"What—no wallet?" The first man sounded angry and disbelieving.

"Yeah, get one wallet," the second voice replied, "but no get cash, bruddah."

Eddie's body tensed. Something his attacker had said was *wrong*. Then the third man swore, and Eddie felt the toe of a heavy boot sharply kicking his ribs. "*Lolo!* Stupid!" the man yelled. Eddie cried out in agony.

Then, through a throbbing red haze of pain, Eddie thought he heard the first man call out, "Bruddah, *no*! He say no hurt 'em!"

After that, Eddie heard several new voices and the sounds of booted feet pounding toward them. His arms were released, and his three attackers fled.

Several pairs of hands pulled Eddie to his

feet. He blinked, trying to focus on the faces of his rescuers. He was pretty sure they must be the Kula'i Street Knights. To his surprise, they all wore hats with the brims pulled down. Their collars were pulled up. Eddie couldn't get a good look at any of them.

Eddie felt his wallet being thrust into his hand. But before he could say anything, the four men turned away and took off running.

Eddie started to run after them, but the pain in his side was too great. Instead, he limped off toward the Kalihi Medical Clinic to have his aching ribs examined.

While the nurse was treating him, Eddie realized that he was still holding his wallet. Apparently his cop's training had taken over—because he was holding it carefully by the sides. That way, any fingerprints would be preserved. After asking for a plastic bag, he slipped the wallet inside.

Eddie's ego had been bruised worse than his ribs. It was embarrassing for a cop to get mugged. Eddie couldn't even give a description of his attackers. His only hope was that a set of prints could be lifted from the wallet.

After he left the clinic, Eddie dropped off his wallet at the station. Sgt. Amosa listened grimly to Eddie's story.

"This has gone too far," the sergeant growled. "Whatever you're working on—give it to someone else. I want you to find these muggers *now*, Eddie. And the Street Knights, too."

Eddie nodded. Lately he'd let his feelings get in the way of his training. Time to start thinking like a cop again.

Eddie started listing things he knew about the Street Knights. It was a short list! His thoughts wandered back to the incident the night before. The muggers had spoken in the local dialect—Pidgin English. That meant they'd been raised in Hawaii. Eddie figured there was a good chance they had criminal records.

"No get cash!" his attacker had said. But Eddie *did* have some `money. He remembered hurriedly stuffing change from a $50.00

bill into his jeans pocket. The mugger had searched him. The guy *couldn't* have missed the money! It wasn't much, but far worse crimes had been committed for less.

Nothing had been stolen from Auntie Malia or Mr. Fernandez, either.

Alarm bells began going off in Eddie's head. "Maybe they aren't after money," he thought. "So what *are* they after?"

Then he remembered something else. After Eddie had been kicked, the third man had cried out, "He say no hurt 'em."

Who had told them not to hurt anyone? Auntie Malia and Mr. Fernandez hadn't been injured, either. Was this a pattern?

Eddie went out to talk to more of the muggers' victims. Within a few hours he realized that not one person had lost anything of value or been hurt.

When he got back to the station, Eddie stopped at the lab. The technician had been able to lift only one clear print. The good news was, they had a match.

"Russell 'Poi Dog' Leong," the tech said.

He handed Eddie a computer print-out of Poi Dog's offenses. The guy had been in and out of trouble since he was a kid. Eddie grinned as he gazed at the photo. Now he could make an arrest.

Then Eddie was struck with another thought. He hadn't gotten a clear look at either the muggers *or* the Knights. Which side was Poi Dog on?

■ ■ ■

The trouble was, Poi Dog could not be found. The cops circulated his picture throughout the neighborhood. Two people identified him as a mugger—but two others identified him as a Knight. Had they made a mistake? Or was something else going on?

Over the next week, the number of muggings increased. Soon two crimes were being committed at almost the same time. The cops had their hands full taking so many statements, analyzing evidence, and making reports.

Then some of the victims were actually

robbed. Oddly enough, these were victims who *couldn't* be rescued because the Knights were already busy elsewhere. Things were getting nasty on the streets of Kalihi.

One afternoon Eddie found himself with some free time on his hands. He'd canceled soccer practice to have his ribs checked. But the doctor had had an emergency at the last minute. The nurse had to reschedule Eddie's appointment.

Eddie wondered what to do with this unexpected mini-vacation. He hadn't had much time off in weeks. He could go back to the station and finish up some paperwork. Or . . . Eddie scanned the blue sky and grinned to himself. "Go to the beach!" he thought happily.

As he headed for his car, Eddie saw a group of people outside Mr. Chang's grocery store. Suddenly, all thoughts of the beach vanished.

He heard loud, angry voices as he approached the group. Mr. Fernandez and Mr. Chang were in the middle of the crowd arguing.

"I tell you, *no!*" Mr. Chang's mouth tightened into a thin angry line. "Once we start, where does it end?"

"Hey, it's just like insurance," Mr. Fernandez roared. "Listen, old man, no be *lolo*. Times change. Wake up! We pay or else."

Eddie worked his way through the crowd. When the two men saw him, they fell silent. Both of them were red-faced and short of breath.

Eddie gazed from one furious face to the other. "Hey! What's going on here?" he asked the men in a calm voice.

Neither man looked Eddie in the eye.

"What are you two fighting about?" Eddie asked. "Listen—you guys have been friends for a long time, right?"

Both men shrugged. Mr. Chang started to go back into the store, but Eddie put his hand on the old man's arm. "You need to tell me what this is about," he said. "Come on. Who is asking you to pay? And for what?"

Mr. Chang shook off Eddie's hand. "You better ask *him*," he said, nodding at Mr. Fernandez. "I got work to do." He stormed back into the store.

Before the door closed, Eddie looked inside the store. He stared in shock at the mess. It looked like a hurricane had hit! Cans had rolled onto the floor. Bags of flour had been split open, their contents spread across the worn linoleum like snow. Pineapples and ripe mangoes were smashed into pulp. "Who did that?" Eddie exclaimed.

"Who you think?" In his anger, Mr. Chang reverted back to Pidgin.

Mrs. Chang came out of the dark interior. Her eyes were red and swollen from crying. "Those punks came in here, tore the place up," she sobbed. "Lucky they no hurt us, just make one awfulmess. Then the Street Knights get here—but too late. They say they can't stop all the crimes. So now, they only going to protect people who pay."

Eddie froze. *"Pay?"* he echoed. "Did they say how much?"

Mr. Chang shrugged. "Not too much. But how come I have to pay anyone? How come you cops can't find those punks? How come—"

Eddie stopped listening. He fished change out of his pocket and headed for the payphone on the corner. He called the station and reported the crime.

While he waited for uniformed cops to arrive, Eddie asked himself another question. *Why hadn't the cops been able to locate the muggers and the Knights?* It was a question that had bothered him for days. How could both the criminals and the Knights appear out of thin air and then disappear without a trace?

The crimes didn't fit a pattern. Neither did the criminals. And neither did the Kulaʻi Street Knights, for that matter.

Eddie got an idea. He grabbed the phone book and flipped through the pages. All the streets on Oahu were listed in the phone book, along with their zip codes. Eddie ran his finger down the columns. It was just as he suspected—there was no Kulaʻi

Street listed.

Eddie deposited more change and called the city office to double-check on Honolulu street names. With so much construction going on all over the island, it was possible that the phone book wasn't up to date. But his suspicion was confirmed. There was no Kula‘i Street anywhere on the island!

Eddie headed for Auntie Malia's house. As he neared the door, he smelled the spicy scent of freshly baked mango bread. He'd come at a good time! Sure enough, Auntie was taking steamy brown loaves out of the oven. When she saw Eddie, she grinned and greeted him warmly. *"Hele mai ‘ai,* Eddie boy," she told him. "Come, eat."

Eddie bit into chunks of fresh mango and juicy raisins in the warm bread. Then, after a moment, he said, "Auntie, what does the word *Kula‘i* mean?"

Auntie spoke fluent Hawaiian. "It means 'to push over,'" she said. "It can also mean 'to knock down' or 'overthrow.' I figured it meant they were knocking down crime in our neighborhood."

"I don't think so," Eddie said softly. "I think it means overthrowing the people, knocking down the residents, pushing over your neighbors."

He told Auntie about what Mr. Fernandez called "paying insurance." "But *I* call it extortion," he said.

Auntie gasped. "How you going to find those guys, Eddie?"

"I've been looking in the wrong place," Eddie said. "Now it's time to expand the search." He carried his plate to the sink. "And something else—" he said. "I'm going to call for another neighborhood meeting, Auntie. Will you help me get everyone together?"

Malia nodded.

■ ■ ■

That evening Eddie again faced a sea of angry faces. But this time he was ready for their questions.

"From the beginning," he told his listeners,

"I felt there was something wrong about the Knights. You know the old saying: If something *seems* too good to be true, it probably is. I kept asking myself *why* these Knights would come to Kalihi to rescue people. What would *they* get out of it?"

Now the listeners' faces mirrored confusion and puzzlement.

Eddie explained how they had identified Poi Dog as a mugging suspect. "The strange part is that some of you fingered Poi Dog as a mugger and some as a Knight."

He heard a rumble of bewildered conversation. "That's when I began to suspect that the Street Knights and the muggers are all part of the same group," he went on.

His listeners gasped in surprise.

"Those dramatic rescues were part of a performance for your benefit," Eddie explained. "You were supposed to feel so grateful to the Knights that you'd be willing to pay for their services later."

"But that's *pupule*—crazy!" Mr. Fernandez exclaimed.

Eddie shook his head. "Think about it. For a few days, every time someone was mugged, the Knights were right there. Nothing was ever stolen, and no one was hurt! *How convenient!*"

No one in the crowd could miss the sarcasm in his tone.

"Then the number of muggings shot up. That's when the extortion game kicked in. From now on, if you want the Knights to watch over your home or business, you have to pay! Right?"

Several people winced at hearing the word "extortion." Eddie nodded. "But it's not insurance," he said. "It's *blackmail!* The Knights and the muggers are on the same side."

He saw the shocked expressions on the faces staring at him.

"Believe it or not," Eddie said, "the cops have been investigating all along. But it takes *time* to build a solid case if we want to make an arrest that will stick. We don't want these jerks out on bail! We want them locked up just as much as you do."

He saw that several residents were nodding now. They knew Eddie was right.

To get their full attention, Eddie waited until everyone was quiet. "Once we finally tracked down Poi Dog, we put a tail on him. He led us to other members of the gang and to a career crook—the so-called brains behind this extortion scheme. Most of them were arrested earlier this evening, but Poi Dog managed to slip through our fingers."

Everyone's eyes widened. Eddie felt a certain amount of satisfaction when their mouths opened in surprise.

"But that doesn't mean it's all over," he went on. "When one set of criminals moves out, another gang moves in. You can still be victimized. Isn't it time you decided to turn things around?"

"Are you going to talk about that Neighborhood Watch program again?" Mrs. Apana asked.

Eddie nodded. "If we work *together*, we can make the neighborhood safe. You can help by forming a Neighborhood Watch, or—"

He heard a low rumble of grumbling, but he pressed on. *"Or,"* he said in a louder tone, "—you can go on paying blackmail money to a bunch of thugs. Which would you prefer?"

It wasn't a tough choice for the people to make. Then, as Eddie was scanning the faces in the crowd, he suddenly saw a familiar figure slip into the shadows at the back of the crowd.

"Time to bring this cockroach into the light," Eddie thought angrily. He jumped off the stage and thrust his way through the crowd. "Hey, Poi Dog!" Eddie shouted. "I want to talk to you."

Poi Dog broke from the shadows. He ran toward the door—but several bystanders grabbed him.

"Watch it, bruddah!" Poi Dog snarled. "I'm a Street Knight. I'm a hero. I'm—"

"I know what you are," Eddie said with a grin. "You're under arrest."

After Poi Dog was taken away, Eddie

turned back to the crowd of residents. "You just took the first step toward winning back your streets," he told them. "How does that feel?"

Their cheers and laughter were all the answer he needed.

After-Reading Wrap-Up

1. Would you like to have Eddie as a cop in your neighborhood? Give two reasons why or why not.

2. At one point in the story, the neighbors say the Street Knights are doing a better job than the cops. What made them feel this way?

3. Name two details about the Street Knights that made Eddie suspicious of them.

4. Did it seem believable to you that the Street Knights and the thugs were the same guys?

5. Did the story's ending seem reasonable to you? Why or why not?

6. Was the story more interesting because it took place in Hawaii? Give a detailed answer.